By Lynn Hodges & Sue Buchanan

A Song of God's Love

Illustrated By John Bendall-Brunello

Angels
Watching Over Me

zonderkidz

zonderkidz
The children's group
of Zondervan

www.zonderkidz.com

Editor: Amy De Vries
Art direction: Laura Maitner-Mason

Illustrations used in this book were created with watercolors.
The body text for this book is set in Gararond.

Printed in China

05 06 07 08 09 /LPC/ 10 9 8 7 6 5 4 3 2 1

The Lord will command his angels
to take good care of you.
Psalm 91:11

On the day that God made you the angels stood by,
They giggled and kissed you and then gave a sigh:

Oh, how can we help you? What can we do
To keep this child safe and trusting in you?

God told them his plan on that special day—
They would watch you and keep you at work
and at play.

God, thank you for angels that watch over me,
For keeping me safe from the things I can't see.
For all of my lifetime, I'll rest with this thought—
There are angels around me. God loves me a lot!

What is an angel and what are they for?
I know that they guard me: I wish I knew more.

Do they laugh when I laugh?
Do they cry when I'm sad?

Do they sleep when I sleep?
Do they smile when I'm glad?

What is an angel?

Are they big?

Are they small?

Do they ju^mp cloud to cloud?

Do they come when I call?

I think they play harps—

And at Christmas, they sing.

God, thank you for angels that watch over me,
For keeping me safe from the things I can't see.
For all of my lifetime, I'll rest with this thought—
There are angels around me. God loves me a lot!

What is an angel? Are they here day and night?
Do they cheer, do they clap, when I do what is right?

When I'm thinking of saying what should not be said
Do they hear the same "shush" that I hear in my head?

God, thank you for angels that watch over me,
For keeping me safe from the things I can't see.
For all of my lifetime, I'll rest with this thought—
There are angels around me. God loves me a lot!

Do they keep me from danger—

From taking a chance?

When I'm thinking of going where I shouldn't go
Do they cartwheel on rainbows, when I wisely choose "no."

God, thank you for angels that watch over me,
For keeping me safe from the things I can't see.
For all of my lifetime, I'll rest with this thought—
There are angels around me. God loves me a lot!

There are angels around us.
God loves us a lot!